The Exsanguinist

Direction artistique : Jamie Keenan
Mise en page : MCP

Enregistrements, montage et mixage : Studio Corby
Texte lu par Les Clack

« Le photocopillage, c'est l'usage abusif et collectif de la photocopie sans autorisation des auteurs et des éditeurs.
Largement répandu dans les établissements d'enseignement, le photocopillage menace l'avenir du livre, car il met en danger son équilibre économique. Il prive les auteurs d'une juste rémunération.
En dehors de l'usage privé du copiste, toute reproduction totale ou partielle de cet ouvrage est interdite. »
« La loi du 11 mars 1957 n'autorisant, au terme des alinéas 2 et 3 de l'article 41, d'une part, que les copies ou reproductions strictement réservées à l'usage privé du copiste et non destinées à une utilisation collective » et, d'autre part, que les analyses et les courtes citations dans un but d'exemple et d'illustration, « toute représentation ou reproduction intégrale, ou partielle, faite sans le consentement de l'auteur ou de ses ayants droit ou ayants cause, est illicite. » (alinéa 1er de l'article 40) – « Cette représentation ou reproduction, par quelque procédé que ce soit, constituerait donc une contrefaçon sanctionnée par les articles 425 et suivants du Code pénal. »

© Les Éditions Didier, Paris, 2010 - ISBN 978-2-278-06857-9 - ISSN 2114-1304
Achevé d'imprimer en octobre 2017 par JOUVE Numérique - Dépôt légal : 6857/02
Imprimé en France

The Exsanguinist
R.N. Morris

didier

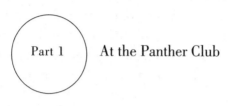

Part 1   At the Panther Club

I

"It's not as easy as you think to kill someone."

If it was Silas Quinn's intention to silence his companions with a remark, he achieved his objective spectacularly. And yet, there was something about his gaze that suggested he had not spoken simply for effect. His eyes, as he stared into the fire, had an isolated intensity. He appeared deadly serious.

"Good heavens, Quinn!" cried one of his fellows at last, the nervously jovial Lord Toby Marchbanks. "You speak as if you know what you are talking about!"

Lord Toby's laughter was forced, and betrayed a touch of fear. In his late thirties, his figure was still impressively youthful, but his good looks were diminished by a certain weakness about the mouth, which fell on one side, in a way which suggested a secret vice. He sat forward on his leather armchair and looked around hopefully for support. It seemed he was uneasy about confronting Quinn alone. Perspiration glistened on his forehead. He gulped down the large glass of brandy and soda that had just been served to him by one of the Panther Club waiters.

In answer to Lord Toby's nervous observation, Quinn's voice was peculiarly devoid of humour. "Naturally. I am not in the habit of talking about things of which I have no knowledge."

"Now, now!" came the first voice in a sceptical chorus. "Steady on!" "Surely not!" "But you mean to say?"

"I mean to say precisely what I said," cut in Quinn emphatically, silencing their incredulity. "It is not as easy as you think to kill someone."

"Be careful, my friend. If I did not know you better, I would think you were confessing to murder."

The warning – with its assumption of a friendship that did not exist – came from the oldest of the group, the Right Honourable Sir Michael Esslyn, Member of Parliament. A thin, pale-skinned man with dark hair and concave cheeks, he watched Silas Quinn closely, with an intensity of expression that mirrored Quinn's own. The trace of a smile curled on Sir Michael's lips, like a snake finding repose on the branch of a tree.

Quinn did not smile. "But you do not know me at all," he observed, with a cold insistence on the factual. "We are not friends, as you suggested."

"Except to say, we are members of the same club. Surely that counts for something?"

Quinn's contemptuous shrug suggested he did not agree.

II

The Panther Club was one of the oldest of London's gentlemen's clubs, founded in 1764 by a group of aristocrats who had been expelled *en masse* from Boodle's for releasing a wild panther in that club's confines. The escapade had resulted in the dismemberment of one of the club's servants, together with the deaths by heart attack of several of the older members. From its origins, therefore, the Panther Club had a reputation for the extreme imprudence of its members. It is interesting to note that the aristocrats who introduced the panther into Boodle's never faced any criminal charges: ejection from their club was considered punishment enough.

It was one hundred and fifty years later, in the spring of 1914, that Silas Quinn offered his strange comment to a small group of men gathered in one of the club's oak-panelled rooms. The intervening years had not diminished the Panther Club's reputation for wildness, although the transgressions embarked upon these days resulted in fewer hospitalisations (leaving aside those caused by certain maladies which were peculiarly endemic among the club's members). Some members, such as Sir Michael, succeeded in maintaining a public air of respectability. But many openly courted scandal, to such an extent that they would not have been welcome in any other gentlemen's club, or in general society for that matter. Such men were always warmly welcomed at the Panther Club.

One of the club's quainter traditions was to keep a live panther caged in the foyer. It was not unknown for certain of the younger members, when drunk, to challenge one another to enter the cage for a *tête à tête* with Bertie. (The club's original panther had been called Bertie, and every one of his successors, male or female, had gone by the same name.)

To 'dine with the panther' (recollecting a phrase of the club's great hero Oscar Wilde) was considered by some members to be a rite of passage, but it is not true that it was ever part of any formal initiation ceremony on joining the club. The rumour alone, however, was sufficient to deter the faint-hearted from even applying for membership.

In fact, the current Bertie was well-fed and semi-tame, and so inclined to tolerate these human intrusions provided his guest showed due respect, and offered a morsel of raw steak by way of rent. Indeed, he was so docile a creature that he often simply cast a disdainful glance at the would-be daredevil before settling his head back down on his front legs to resume his siesta.

III

"So you have...? Murdered?"

Was there a glimmer of respect in the Marquess of Roachford's tone, or was it perhaps a morbid excitement? Known as Pinky to his friends, and wearing a lilac lounge suit, the Marquess of Roachford was the most dandified of the group. The monocle dropped from his eye and his face flushed a shade of pink that justified his soubriquet.

Quinn considered for a moment before replying, "I have certainly given it a great deal of thought."

"Ah, I see," said Sir Michael, a hint of disappointment entering his voice. "You are a theoretician of murder, rather than a practitioner?"

"Why is it you people always rephrase what I have said in words that are not my own? Can you not see that you will inevitably alter my meaning?" The heat of Quinn's response was disproportionate, and therefore provoked general disapproval. It was rather ungentlemanly on his part to become so agitated.

"My dear fellow, I am only trying to understand you better."

"Is my meaning not clear enough? What is it about what I have said that you do not understand? *It is not as easy as you think to kill someone.*"

"But none of us has suggested that it is easy!" pointed out Lord Toby, with his usual nervous laugh.

"And it is not so much what you have said that causes consternation as the manner in which you said it," said the last member of the group, who until now had remained silent. This was the Hungarian, Count Lázár Erdélyi, who was there as a guest of the Marquess of Roachford. "It is almost as if you are defending the practice of murder on a point of honour."

"Perhaps I am."

"Well, I am not an exemplary moralist myself, but I rather think you should not." Count Erdélyi had been educated at Eton and spoke English impeccably, with no trace of an accent. He presented a strangely symmetrical figure, particularly about the face: his hair and moustaches were centrally parted and held precisely in place with pomade and wax respectively.

"Even to conceive of killing someone, and then to formulate a plan for how one may put the intention into action... that in itself requires..." Quinn broke off, searching for the right word. "Character," he opted for at last. "But to proceed with it! To turn the intention into an act! That is something beyond character – that is evidence of a superhuman greatness!"

"My dear fellow, you will have to do better than that," said Sir Michael with an air of lassitude. "The crime of murder is rather more common than you suggest. And even some quite unexceptionable people have proven themselves capable of homicide. Desperate husbands and ambitious wives. Members of the lower orders are particularly prone to it – all it takes is a few glasses of strong liquor for them to overcome whatever minuscule scruples they might have. Why, even the middle classes have indulged in it on occasion."

"All these people whom you so disdain have proven themselves gods."

"Oh, now you really are going too far, Quinn!" objected Lord Toby. His mouth twitched into an uncomfortable smirk, as his eyes looked nervously about.

"Have you ever tried to kill someone?" demanded Quinn in response. "I mean you yourself, with your own hands?" Quinn held his hands in front of his face, and examined the splayed fingers with a look of horror.

"Have *you*?"

A violent spasm convulsed Silas Quinn. He looked into the young lord's eyes as if into an abyss into which he was in danger of falling. "Yes, of course."

IV

At that moment there was a sound like a gun being fired. Everyone, except for Quinn, jumped in shock. When they realised it was simply a coal exploding in the fireplace, laughter released their tension. Quinn alone remained serious. His face had a dejected look to it.

"I failed," he said.

"You failed?" said Pinky, turning from the fire which had distracted them all from what Quinn had been saying. "At what?"

"At killing."

All eyes turned on Quinn. No one spoke. Their attention was focussed entirely upon him again. They waited for him to continue.

"It happened many years ago. I was a student of medicine at the time. I never completed my studies. It was said that I became ill, that I suffered a nervous breakdown. Perhaps that is the truth. I do not remember. Before it happened, I was lodging in a guest house in Camden. And it was there that I met the man I determined to kill. He was also a student, and everything that I was not: handsome, popular, athletic. But superficial: a man of surface, an insincere, empty man. A bubble of a man. Surely it should not have been so hard to pop him? The landlady had a daughter. My enemy had an easy way with the opposite sex and charmed the girl into an affectionate relationship. But I saw what he was really like. I could not allow him to... I loved her, you see. Genuinely, not like he did. My love for her was total, absolute, pure – and deep. There was no one else for me. And so, I decided that the only solution to my problem was to eliminate my rival. But I tell you, it is not as easy as you think to kill someone." There was something desperate in Quinn's eyes as he scanned his listeners.

"Did you try awfully hard?" asked Pinky.

"First I had to decide upon the place where I would kill him – the scene of the crime, as it were. I did not want to do it at the lodging house. That would incriminate me too much. I needed to choose a neutral place, one not associated with me, and yet somewhere to which I could lure him. It had to be a lonely spot, nowhere overlooked. And I had to be sure that I would not be interrupted. I decided to write a note in the girl's name, in which she promised to give herself to him completely if he would meet her by the canal, beneath the bridge near Camden Lock after dark. In her name, I commanded him to destroy the note once he had read it and to say nothing of the assignation to anyone.

My medical studies were not so far advanced that I had learnt how to ease suffering or cure disease. But I had learnt enough to know how to inflict a fatal wound quickly and efficiently. My plan was to cut his throat with a barber's razor and then push him off the towpath into the canal. The body would inevitably be found, but there would be nothing linking me to it. No one knew of my love for the landlady's daughter, not even the object of my affections herself. It would be assumed that he was the victim of a violent robbery that had gone too far."

"And so, how did this melodrama play out?"

"As I think you can guess, I could not do it. As soon as I heard his voice, calling out the girl's name in the darkness, instead of the hatred I thought I would feel, I... I felt only horror. Horror at what I was about to do. I imagined the blade of the razor touching his throat. In my imagination, the skin of his throat was impossibly resistant, like leather. The blade would not penetrate it. As I could not imagine myself cutting his throat, I could not go through with the murder. I threw the razor into the canal and ran."

"A lucky escape, for you as much as for him," said Sir Michael.

"But why could I not go through with it? It was not compassion. I still hated him. I still wanted him dead. That night, I dreamed of killing him. I was able to accomplish in my dreams what I had not managed to do in reality. The supernaturally sharp blade cut through his skin effortlessly. The blood spurted out from his neck. The canal filled with scarlet liquid, rising higher and higher until it inundated the ground around my feet. I looked in horror at the boy I had killed – for he was just a boy – and saw that he was both dead and not dead at the same time. The life had gone from his eyes, but he continued to stand up, and was even able to move: but strangely, like an automaton. Suddenly, the cut in his neck stopped spurting blood. Terror gripped my heart. I knew that the cut was about to speak to me. Its sides opened like the lips of a mouth."

"Good heavens! What did it say?" asked Sir Michael.

Quinn buried his face in his hands and shook his head. When he removed his hands, his face was flushed. "I awoke from that vile dream and jumped screaming from my bed. I ran through the lodging house, naked and screaming, until I fell unconscious outside the door of my hated rival. When I regained consciousness, I was in a hospital bed. I did not find peace then and I have not found it since. Sometimes I think that the only way I will ever find peace is if I hunt him down and kill him."

V

"But why are you telling us all this?" Count Erdélyi yawned to show that he was not really interested in a reply.

"Because I believe each of you is capable of the very thing I am not."

"Really?" said Sir Michael, simply raising an eyebrow instead of exclaiming in outrage. "You consider us to be a gang of murderers?"

Quinn turned on Sir Michael impassively. "There is a war coming. As a member of the government, Sir Michael, you will be responsible for the deaths of tens of thousands of young men. You will agree to it without hesitation. You will justify it as a political necessity. But it will be murder. Your pen as you sign the order will be dipped in blood."

Sir Michael turned his head to one side sceptically, but said nothing.

Lord Toby's mouth twitched affably. "I don't think I could kill someone any more than you could, old fellow," he protested.

"Does the name Sophie Armstrong mean nothing to you?"

A palpable tension seized the company.

"I say, Quinn," warned Sir Michael. "There's no reason to talk about that. Remember the club rules."

But Quinn gave no indication of being aware of the club rules, continuing: "Quite a scandal, wasn't it? The abortion, her death at the hands of a medical charlatan. It couldn't have come at a worse time for you. Just as you were having your first exhibition. In those days you still had artistic ambitions, I believe. An exhibition filled with paintings of the model whose death you had caused. Wasn't it you who paid for the operation?"

"You cannot call that murder." Lord Toby answered, "It was unfortunate, but not murder."

"But there were rumours about women who had died as a result of his ministrations, were there not? Did you not know that he was an alcoholic and a drug-addict? Had you not seen the disgusting premises in which he carried out his operations? You caused her death as certainly as if you had pointed a gun at her head and pulled the trigger."

"What choice did I have?"

"Please, there is no need to justify yourself to me! Don't you see, I admire you! I merely want you to admit what you did, what you were capable of. What you are!"

"But I did not want her dead. That was not my intention."

"You wanted her out of your life. You had ambitions. Her continuing existence with an illegitimate child could only have been an encumbrance to you. Her death was more than convenient, it was necessary – it was the duty that you owed your Art. What kind of a muse would she be with distended skin and hanging breasts? What a pity that you subsequently abandoned your artistic aspirations and turned instead to... other distractions."

"I discovered that I had no talent. It was better to realise that when I was still young."

"Oh, was it that? I thought it was the fact that all your potential clients – your society friends, in other words – deserted you. The exhibition was a disaster. That must have been painful for you. But the pain diminishes with time, does it not? Particularly when assisted by an opium habit. It was, after all, in a Limehouse opium den that you met the doctor concerned."

"I have cured myself of my addiction," protested Lord Toby, his thin lips closed tightly together.

"I congratulate you. It is not an easy thing to do, to open yourself to pain again. But soon there will be pleasure too, for I hear that you are to marry. Your fiancée is Lady Jane Wingarde, I believe. What a spectacular couple you will make! It is clear that you did the right thing eliminating Sophie Armstrong all those years ago."

Lord Toby's expression closed in on itself. Once more, Sir Michael spoke on his behalf: "You should know, Quinn, that we do not allow such talk in the Panther Club. We do not judge one another here."

Silas Quinn widened his eyes, as if this information came as a great surprise to him.

VI

"And what of us?" said Count Erdélyi, gesturing to include his friend the Marquess of Roachford. "I am interested to hear why you think we are capable of murder."

"You will have read of the recent series of murders that are exercising our police here in the capital," answered Quinn.

"The Exsanguinist!" hissed Pinky. Once again, the monocle fell from his right eye.

"Yes. That is indeed how the newspapers have referred to the man responsible for these crimes." Quinn turned back to Count Erdélyi. "I believe,

Count, that your presence here in London has something to do with that case."

"Would you care to explain what you mean by that?"

"Your name... Erdélyi. It means Transylvanian."

"I am aware of that."

"You are a Transylvanian Hungarian."

"What of it?"

"There are stories of creatures in Transylvania who drink the blood of others."

"I am familiar with such stories. Do you believe me to be a vampire?" Count Erdélyi asked mockingly. His shoulders shook with laughter. But strangely there was no humour in his eyes.

"On the contrary, I know you are here in London at the request of Scotland Yard, who are now prepared to consider the possibility that these crimes have been perpetrated by one of those very creatures. They hope to recruit you in the hunt for and destruction of the Exsanguinist. You have performed such work before."

"I am sure I don't know what you are talking about. And even if I did know what you are talking about, it is nonsense. These murders are not, in point of fact, consistent with the behaviour of the vampire of Transylvanian tradition. The bloodlessness of this man's victims requires nothing more supernatural than a bucket. Have you never seen a pig being drained of its blood, Mr Quinn?"

Quinn narrowed his eyes as though he were considering a response, which he declined to give.

"But what about me?" said Pinky, petulant it seemed at being left till last. "I couldn't hurt a fly."

Quinn turned slowly to face the Marquess. "All of the Exsanguinist's twenty-one reported victims have been young men of the labouring classes. Is it not true that you have a predilection for such youths?"

"I have a predilection for beauty! What gentleman doesn't?"

"In any case, you have a talent for persuading young men to go with you..."

"There is no talent. It is simply a question of offering them sufficient money."

"Pinky could not possibly be the Exsanguinist!" objected Count Erdélyi.

"You're right," agreed Quinn. "I do not in fact believe that the Marquess of Roachford is the Exsanguinist. However, I would like to ask him about a youth called Tommy Venables, a junior employee at the telegram office."

"How do you know Tommy Venables?" demanded Pinky darkly.

"Let's just say he was a friend of mine."

Pinky's nose twitched as if assailed by an unpleasant odour. "You should choose your friends more carefully. Tommy Venables is a nasty little swine."

"Yes, and more to the point, a blackmailer." Quinn met the suspicious, questioning glances of the others. "Oh yes, I warned him about it. I knew it would get him into trouble." Quinn turned again to Pinky. "He threatened to create a scandal, did he not? How convenient that he is now numbered among the Exsanguinist's victims!"

"But you said yourself that you do not believe me to be the Exsanguinist."

"That's true. What's also true is that when a prolific killer such as the Exsanguinist is at large, others take advantage of the situation. In some instances, it is almost as if there is a contagion of killing, but more often it is simply a case of opportunism. Let us say there is someone you want to dispose of – a Tommy Venables, for example. Your one particular murder can be hidden in the cloud of general terror and destruction created by one such as the Exsanguinist. Your crime may be mistaken for one of his."

"Be careful, Quinn. You have overstepped the mark. This is outrageous defamation," warned Sir Michael on the Marquess's behalf. Pinky himself remained tight-lipped, his characteristic colour drained from his face.

"But you misunderstand me. I do not say this to condemn the Marquess. And it goes without saying that I would not repeat any of this to anyone other than ourselves. This is all, as it were, between friends."

"Well, my *friends*," began Count Erdélyi, deliberately repeating and emphasising Quinn's word. "All this talk of bloodshed is making me hungry." He patted both arms down and rose from his armchair with an air of resolution. "I take it that the food is acceptable here."

"Are you running away from the discussion?" said Quinn.

"Not at all. You are welcome to continue it in the dining room."

"No thank you. I am following a strict and rather unusual diet at the moment. I find the sight and smell of ordinary food nauseating. It has been interesting talking to you gentlemen. I trust we will meet again. In fact, I am sure of it."

With that, Silas Quinn was gone.

VII

"What a strange man, if you don't mind me saying," said Sir Michael pensively.

"I don't mind!" answered Lord Toby. "I only met the fellow tonight."

"Then he did not come with you?"

"No. I thought he came with you."

"So is he a friend of yours, Pinky?" inquired Sir Michael.

"He is hardly my type!"

"And he cannot have been the count's guest, because the count is here as *your* guest."

"I have never met him before," confirmed Count Erdélyi.

"And yet he seemed to know a lot about you, Lázár!" teased Pinky.

Count Erdélyi appeared unimpressed by the observation. "He seemed to know a lot about us all," he murmured.

"Why, the impertinent fellow just attached himself to us!" cried Lord Toby.

"Is he a member of the club?" wondered Sir Michael. "I do not remember seeing him before tonight."

 Part 2   De Profundis

I

NEXT MORNING, a black Unic taxi came to a halt on the Thames Embankment. The building towering over it was granite grey at street level, and red brick in the upper floors. High tourelles at each corner gave it something of the air of a Scottish castle: a flamboyant touch of the architect's, perhaps suggested by the building's name, for this was New Scotland Yard, the headquarters of the London Metropolitan Police since 1890. The clock tower of the Palace of Westminster rose up next to it. The hands on the clock face indicated that Big Ben was about to strike eleven. Count Lázár Erdélyi – for it was he who jumped down from the taxi just as the great bell began to ring majestically – was on time for his meeting.

After presenting his identity papers at reception, and asking for the 'Special Crimes Department', he was escorted to a room high in the building by a uniformed copper. He realised it was under the roof because one wall was angled and he had climbed many flights of stairs to reach it. He was breathless and his heart was beating hard.

He was invited to take a seat and await 'The Inspector'. A moment later the door to the room opened and his heart seemed to stop altogether.

II

"You!"

"You did not expect to see me again so soon, Count Erdélyi?"

"What the devil are you doing here, Quinn?"

"Detective Inspector Quinn, actually."

"You? A policeman?"

"Yes. Is it so strange?"

"But you didn't say."

"I apologise. I could not be frank last night for reasons that will become apparent." Quinn was accompanied into the room by two other men; all were wearing plain clothes. "These gentlemen are fellow officers of mine, Detectives Inchball and

McAdam. I have briefed them fully about you and your particular expertise."

Quinn's two sombre-faced colleagues nodded to Count Erdélyi. Something about their expressions suggested that they neither trusted nor approved of him.

The count's mouth hung open. "After all that you said last night! About your fellow lodger... and your murderous intentions towards him!"

"All that was true. What I omitted to relate was the sequel to that episode. I had glimpsed the potential for darkness in the heart of every man. What had induced my breakdown was the realisation that I was capable of contemplating such crimes, and that the contemplation of a crime is only a step away from committing it. The mental and physical collapse I suffered was my body's way of preventing me from carrying out my intention. The body acted as policeman to the soul, which had become corrupt and malign. I had perceived how easy it might be for a man – who had until then believed himself to be someone decent – to become capable of the most atrocious of crimes. I determined to use that perception for good, and joined the Metropolitan Police, where I soon revealed an aptitude for investigative work. That is my story."

"But why did you not say this last night? You were deliberately engaging in mystifications, you know."

"We will come to that," said Quinn. "But first, I would like you to look at this dossier." He handed a beige cardboard folder to the count.

Count Erdélyi raised one eyebrow as he took the folder, breaking the perfect symmetry of his face.

III

Count Erdélyi was shaking as he closed the dossier. He placed it on the table in front of him and pulled his hands away brusquely, as though from something contaminated. His face was drained of blood. Detective Inspector Silas Quinn watched him closely. At last the count spoke, quietly, a slight tremble in his voice: "I did not realise there were so many victims."

"We have kept the full extent of the Exsanguinist's crimes out of the newspapers."

"Why?"

"If people knew how prolific a killer he really is, the panic would be uncontrollable."

"But surely you cannot keep the details secret forever?"

"Not forever. But long enough for us to catch up with him. The trick is to make the killer believe that he is one step ahead of the police, whereas..."

"But he *is* one step ahead of you!" interjected the count with unexpected fury. "More than that! He is a whole ten leagues ahead of you!"

"Tell me one thing, Count Erdélyi, now that you have seen the photographs. Is this the work of a vampire, I mean of the kind that you are used to dealing with?"

A look passed between the two detectives who had accompanied Quinn into the room. One rolled his eyes and the other smirked.

Count Erdélyi pursed his lips disapprovingly. "It is not a Transylvanian vampire, if that's what you mean. The necks of these victims have been cut. A vampire bites, he does not slash. The wounds here are consistent with the action of a sharp blade – a razor, for example, such as the one you once intended to use against your fellow lodger. You know, last night I convinced myself that *you* were the Exsanguinist."

"And I still might be, for all that you know. Due to the magnitude of the crimes, we believe the perpetrator to be a figure of authority, who is able to come and go without provoking suspicion or being challenged."

"The vampire is capable of the same ubiquity, which he achieves through supernatural means."

Detectives Inchball and McAdam shared another moment of sceptical amusement.

Quinn gave a ironic smile. "It was I who insisted upon your participation in this case, you know. Against considerable opposition, I might add. Certain of my colleagues are inclined to reject all mention of the supernatural out of hand."

"I don't blame them. I would do the same in their shoes," confided Count Erdélyi. "You do know that instances of true vampirism are exceedingly rare – and getting rarer. They are a sick and dying race. Besides that, there are those like me who do everything in our power to eradicate them. We are very close to eliminating the entire vampire population of Transylvania."

"My understanding was that the vampire is in fact dead already, and exists in a state of living death. Therefore..."

"Any talk of the vampire's state of existence can only ever be approximate," interrupted the count. "We simply do not know how their organisms operate and endure – sometimes for centuries.

However, it is not in the interest of the true vampire to commit such public crimes as these." The count tapped his clawed fingers down on the dossier. "A vampire's continuance depends on its ability to persuade us that it does not exist – that it is nothing more than a legend." He flashed a warning look that silenced the two sniggering detectives.

VI

The count's clawed hand relaxed and he laid his palm tenderly on the cover of the dossier.

"But do not fear. This is not a vampire in the true sense," he affirmed. "There is no supernatural aspect to this case."

"How can you be so certain?" asked Quinn.

"Because these boys are dead. That is to say, they have stayed dead. They did not join the ranks of the one who attacked them."

Quinn nodded thoughtfully. "There is an interesting detail, shared by all of the victims except one. Did you notice it?"

"You mean the pages?"

"No, we will come to that. I was thinking of something that is more immediately apparent to the eye."

Count Erdélyi frowned quizzically. He opened the dossier again and looked through the photographs of the murdered youths. "They are all very beautiful," he said at last.

"I had in mind the absence of blood on their clothes. That is singular – do you not agree? They had their throats cut. We would expect considerable blood-soaking, unless..."

"Unless they were not wearing these clothes when they were murdered."

"Precisely. Their bodies were perfectly clean too. If they were naked when they were killed, then their bodies must have been washed, and then dressed, before being abandoned. That suggests a ritual aspect to the crimes, does it not?"

"Perhaps. I can think of another reason why their killer might have undressed them."

"Yes, of course. Whatever the reason, this was the case for all the bodies except that of Tommy Venables, whose clothes were covered in his own blood. That is why we are convinced he was not killed by the same perpetrator as the rest."

"You cannot seriously suspect Pinky? Not even of that one murder."

"My dear count, I know myself what any man is capable of. I cannot exclude the Marquess of

Roachford simply because he is a friend of yours. However, I must admit that the singular murder of Tommy Venables concerns me less than the multiple crimes of the Exsanguinist. My instinct is that, for all his public show of decadence, the Marquess of Roachford is not fundamentally an evil man. Feeble, immoral – depraved even. But not evil. If he did murder Tommy Venables, he did so out of desperation. You might say he was forced into it. I feel that he may, if prevailed upon by a good friend, be persuaded to confess. It would be better for him if he did, you know."

"I see."

There was a pause, before Quinn ventured tentatively: "Count Erdélyi?"

"Yes?"

"I have a confession to make. My reason for wanting your association with this case is not solely because of your experience as a vampire-killer. It is equally because you are a friend of the Marquess of Roachford, and because, I believe, you share certain of his tastes."

Count Erdélyi made no reply, except to frown severely at the two detectives with Quinn.

"To return to the pages that you alluded to earlier," continued Quinn. "In the pockets of each victim – except Tommy Venables – there was a page from the American edition of Oscar Wilde's *De Profundis* or, to give it the title that Wilde himself preferred, the *Epistola: In Carcere et Vinculis*. You will know that this was the long letter of recrimination he wrote to his former lover, Lord Alfred Douglas, while he was imprisoned in Reading Jail as a homosexual."

"There is no need to remind me. And yes, that detail did indeed strike me as interesting."

"I thought it would."

"I assure you, Quinn, you are wrong about me. I am an admirer of beauty, that is true, but in the abstract, and from a distance. I have never..."

"Please. We are not here to enquire into that. We are here to catch a monster and you can help us. If you are truly a lover of beauty, then surely you are obliged to fight against beauty's destroyer?"

"Tell me what you would have me do," said Count Erdélyi with quiet resolution.

V

"You may be asking yourself why I was at the Panther Club last night," began Quinn. "And why I chose to pass the evening in the company of your circle of friends."

"I am beginning to suspect you had your reasons."

"The American edition of *De Profundis*, published by G.P. Putnam's Sons, contains material excised from the original English edition, published by Methuen. There is, for example, this sentence: *It was like feasting with panthers; the danger was half the excitement.*"

"In reality, dining with Bertie is usually quite unexciting, I am told."

"The Exsanguinist's victims are in general exactly the type of young working class males favoured by Wilde – the panthers in his analogy. That, I believe, is the significance of the pages placed in their pockets."

"And it was this that led you to the Panther Club?"

"Other clues have led me in other directions. But naturally, the discovery of the pages inspired me to read Wilde's text closely, at which time I became aware of the discrepancies between the two editions. It seemed significant to me that the Putnam's edition had been chosen over the Methuen. In the American edition, the *Epistola: In Carcere et Vinculis* comprises one hundred and twenty-two pages, or sixty-one double-sided leaves. So far, there have been, in fact, forty-nine victims, not counting Tommy Venables. If we are to imagine that he will continue until he has produced a victim for each page, then we may expect another twelve murders."

"But why would anyone do this?"

"On the one hand, it almost seems as if they are taking vengeance for what happened to Oscar Wilde."

"But if that is the case," objected Count Erdélyi, "why choose victims from the section of humanity particularly loved by Wilde?"

"Loved? Perhaps. But how much also he must have suffered at their hands! The letter to Lord Alfred, though he is not of the same social class as the 'panthers', is full of the bitterest reproach. Or perhaps another quotation from Oscar Wilde may be pertinent here. It is from *The Picture of Dorian Gray*." Quinn took out a pocket notebook and found a page in it. *"There were moments when he looked on evil simply as a mode through which he could realise his conception of the beautiful,"* he read.

"You are a very literary gentleman, for a police detective."

"This case has obliged me to take an interest in literary matters, however contrary to my natural inclinations that may be. From what I understand, Oscar Wilde hoped to turn his life into a work of art. It appears that the Exsanguinist hopes to do the same with death. In some ways, we may view the Exsanguinist as a kind of anti-Wilde. An aesthete in his own way, but a dark and terribly destructive one."

"But what about the blood? Or should I say, the lack of it? Have you comprehended the significance of that?"

"If we are facing an aesthete rather than a vampire, then the absence of blood must be symbolic. That is to say, he has not killed them because he wants their blood. He has drained their blood because he wants to say something by it."

"And what, in your opinion, does he want to say?"

"The pages from *De Profundis* are being left out of sequence. I cannot yet interpret the significance of the chosen sequence, if indeed there is any significance to it. It may simply be designed to confuse. However, on the page left in the pocket of the thirty-first victim – who would be at the mid-point of the murder series if he kills one youth for each leaf of Wilde's published letter – a phrase has been underlined." Again Quinn consulted his notebook, though the count had the impression this was not necessary and he knew the sentence he was about to read by heart. "*She goes to the shedding of blood. This sentence also is not in the Methuen edition.*"

"*She?* Who is this *she?*"

"From the context, it is clear that Wilde has in mind a personification of destruction and ruin. There is a sense of this being our destiny – that we cannot escape disaster. If the killings do indeed have a ritualistic aspect, then perhaps the Exsanguinist's shedding of blood is designed to convoke further destruction. Or, to put it another way, to cause an even greater catastrophe."

"Are you suggesting that there is some form of magic at work here?"

"It only need be in the killer's mind. It is enough to say that he considers himself to be engaged in some form of magical operation – a convocation, we might call it. Life imitates Art, they say. And so, through the exercise of his Black Art, he is showing Life the way."

"You have not answered the biggest question of all – why?"

"Pure bloodlust. Do you remember what Wilde

says about Ezzelino da Romano, in *The Picture of Dorian Gray?*"

"No, but I have a feeling that you have it written in that little book of yours."

Quinn did indeed consult his notebook. "*Ezzelin, whose melancholy could be cured only by the spectacle of death, and who had a passion for red blood, as other men have for red wine...*"

Count Erdélyi was silent for several moments as he absorbed all of this. "What has this to do with me?" he asked at last.

"I believe the Exsanguinist is a member of the Panther Club. And having investigated the full list of members, I am convinced he is one of the gentlemen known to you."

Part 3 — Dinner at the Cadogan Hotel

I

"And how would you like your steak, sir?"

"Rare." Count Erdélyi folded the menu and handed it to the waiter. He looked around the Cadogan Hotel restaurant distractedly as the waiter took the orders from the rest of his party. The light from the chandeliers glinted in the crystal glasses and cutlery, and in the jewels worn by the female diners. It found an auditory echo in the murmur of conversation twinkling with discreet laughter. Suddenly, the vulgar cackle of a large woman in a purple dress at a nearby table perturbed the gentle civility of the room. Count Erdélyi grimaced at the sound.

He turned his attention to his neighbour, Sir Michael Esslyn, who seemed to be in something of a dilemma over his main course. "The veal, I think," he finally decided. "And bring us a bottle of Château Ausone, 1900."

"Excellent choice, sir."

Sir Michael's mouth twisted into an ugly snarl as he watched the waiter retreat from the table, bowing as he went. "I do hate it when they do that," he commented.

"I don't like them too servile, either," said Pinky.

"No – I mean, when they congratulate me on my taste. It is the opposite of servility. It is impertinence. Pretentious little..."

"I think he's rather charming, actually." Pinky tracked the waiter with a hungry gaze.

"Really, Pinky, you are incorrigible!" exclaimed Lord Toby, his voice high and over-excited.

"I should have thought dining here at the Cadogan would have a calming effect upon your impulses," added Sir Michael irritably.

"Ah yes... dear Oscar. It's true that the Cadogan does have bittersweet associations: for it was here, of course, that he was arrested. Against the bitterness of Wilde's disgrace, we can set the exquisite sweetness of their raspberry meringue."

Lord Toby grinned vacuously.

Sir Michael shook his head indulgently. "I sometimes think you have no heart."

Pinky gave a regretful smile. "I sometimes wish I had none." He turned to Count Erdélyi. "You are very quiet tonight, Lázár."

"You know my views on the subject."

"One may look but not touch? Why, that's almost puritanical."

"It might do you good to abstain occasionally."

"Abstain? The only thing I can abstain from is abstinence itself."

"Please, Pinky, try as you might, you are no Oscar Wilde. Not in respect of your wit, at least."

"You are in a vile temper, Lázár, and you are ruining everyone else's good humour too."

"I am not myself, I admit it. I don't know why exactly."

"I do," said Pinky. "It is the fault of the very abstinence you advocate!"

Before Count Erdélyi could answer, the wine arrived for Sir Michael to taste. He pursed his lips over his glass as he gently agitated the ruby liquid to release the aroma. There was something sacramental in his demeanour, as if he were the ministering priest and the others were his congregation. A brusque nod of the head signalled his approval, and the wine proceeded to flow.

"The blood of Christ," murmured Count Erdélyi.

II

"*What* did you say, Lázár?" Pinky asked in astonishment. "If I didn't know you better I would swear you had said 'The blood of Christ'! But you are too good a Catholic to blaspheme, and too bad a one to be in earnest. Whatever can you have been thinking?"

"I... Did I really say that? I confess that I have been thinking a lot about religion recently. At times, I feel a great spiritual agitation inside me, as though I am on the point of some crucial decision, like a return to the Church, or – its opposite. I can even imagine taking holy orders. Perhaps it is due to my work, but more and more I have come to believe that there is only good or evil, and one must make a choice."

"You cannot be serious?"

"I am quite serious, but I do not expect you to understand, Pinky. I would only ask you not to mock the sincerity of my spiritual conflict."

"What has brought this on?"

Count Erdélyi shook his head as if to dismiss unwelcome thoughts. "Do you remember that fellow we met at the Panther Club the other night?"

"Quinn. Silas Quinn," furnished Sir Michael with a strange alacrity.

"Yes. That's right. Thank you, Michael. How clever of you to remember. Quinn. Well, I encountered him again."

"A decidedly strange individual – quite sinister," pronounced Sir Michael.

"I didn't like him at all," said Pinky. "I am not surprised the sight of him has vexed you. What did he have to say for himself this time?"

Count Erdélyi seemed not to have heard the question. "Do you remember how he talked about the Exsanguinist? You know, ridiculous as it may sound, I have half-convinced myself that he is the Exsanguinist."

"He professed to be incapable of murder," remarked Sir Michael. "Unlike us," he added drily.

"Did it not strike you that he protested a little too much?"

"That's true!" exclaimed Lord Toby.

"And then there was the dream that he related.

I was recently in Vienna, where I attended a series of interesting talks given by a noted specialist in dream interpretation. I cannot help asking myself what that expert would make of Quinn's dream."

"Was it Dr. Freud?" asked Sir Michael. "I rather fear that he sees phalluses everywhere."

"How wonderful," said Pinky, licking his lips.

III

"It was a disciple of Freud's," admitted Count Erdélyi. "And from what I understand of Freud's theories, Quinn's dream suggests the repression of certain desires. The meaning is clear: that he wished to have sexual relations with the boy and not his landlady's daughter. I believe the words spoken by the wound – which Quinn would not share with us – would make this explicit. The outpouring of blood is nothing less than…"

"Yes, yes," cut in Sir Michael. "I think we can imagine what that is meant to represent."

"None of this could be admitted by Quinn's conflicted psyche," continued Count Erdélyi. "In fact, to suppress the desire, he kills the object of his desire. But only in his dream. He failed to do so in real life. Do you remember what Quinn said to us? That he will not find peace until he has tracked down and killed his former rival. Is it not conceivable that the crimes of the Exsanguinist reflect that intention? But instead of finding and killing the one he loved – who would by now have aged somewhat – he is repeatedly obliterating the idea of him *as he once was*, in the form of other youths."

"It is an interesting theory," said Sir Michael. "Have you shared your thoughts with the police? Didn't Quinn say you are working with Scotland Yard? Though how on earth he would know that is beyond me."

"He did not know it, because it is not true. But if he is the Exsanguinist, he would naturally take an interest in the cases I have worked on in Rumania. With the usual egoism of a maniac, he places himself at the centre of the universe and sees my presence in London as being connected with him and his crimes. Whereas the truth of the matter is I am here to see friends and to attend to one or two business matters. But to answer your question, Michael, no – I have not mentioned my suspicions to the police. It is a terrible thing to accuse any man of murder. I wish to be sure of myself before I proceed along that route."

"That's understandable, but in this case – if he

is the Exsanguinist – do you not feel you have a duty to report your suspicions at the soonest opportunity? He is already responsible for a prodigious number of deaths."

"You forget, I am accustomed to dealing with dangerous monsters. I intend to trap him myself and deliver him to the authorities when I have either extracted a confession from him or have conclusive evidence of his crimes."

"And what if, in the process, you should become a victim of his next crime yourself?"

"I do not intend to let that happen. And besides, as Pinky might put it, I hardly think I am his type."

VI

"It is a dangerous game," pronounced Sir Michael as the first course arrived.

"And what if he's not the Exsanguinist?" It was Lord Toby who raised this objection.

Count Erdélyi regarded him in silence for a moment, as though he had not understood the question. A high, nervous laugh from Lord Toby at last prompted him to reply: "I feel certain that he is. When I encountered him today, some instinct convinced me that he is capable of great evil. What repulsed me most of all was that he seemed to think I was similar to him. He tried to recruit me into a form of collusion."

"In what way?" There was a hint of excitement in Lord Toby's question, as if he too wanted to help.

"He intimated that I might know of places – establishments – where he could meet youths, youths of the sort the Exsanguinist chooses for his victims. It was clear that he wanted me to find fresh boys for him."

"I don't know why he went to you," complained Pinky with a petulant moue.

"Yes, I wondered myself why he chose me. I thought at first that it was simply the accident of our encounter. But I do not believe anything happens accidentally where Quinn is concerned. He must have engineered our meeting. I believe he chose me, rather than you, Pinky – for I think we can all agree you would be the obvious choice – because he sensed the conflicts in my personality. He cannot openly ally himself with someone like you who is so... how shall I put it? ...so extravagantly *Hellenic* in his lifestyle. I am aware that I project a more ambiguous persona. Subconsciously, perhaps, that established some kind of affinity between us in his mind. I can think of no other explanation. He suspects that my tastes cause me a degree of anguish – as they do him. No doubt he imagines that this will make me a more malleable instrument to control. In addition, the fact that he believes me to be a vampire-hunter may have added piquancy to his choice. Perhaps he considers himself to be playing with fire. Alternatively, he may, in fact, be conspiring against himself: deep down he may *want* to be caught. It is not impossible that he has had enough of killing, and sees this as the only way to stop himself."

"Did you agree to help him?" Sir Michael's question had a strangely cautious tone to it.

"No. I rejected his overtures out of hand."

"What purpose was served by that?" wondered Sir Michael.

"None. It was not a ruse. At the time, I genuinely wanted nothing more to do with him. However..." Count Erdélyi produced a visiting card from his pocket. "He forced his card on me. I intend to call upon him. Tonight."

"Are you sure that's wise?" warned Sir Michael.

"I see no reason to wait."

"Do you intend to go alone?" asked Pinky in alarm.

"Yes. It has to be that way. But I want all of you to know where I have gone and whom I shall be meeting. Just in case something happens to me." Count Erdélyi handed the card to Sir Michael. "Please pass it round."

"I see he still lives in Camden," observed Lord Toby, when the card came to him.

"That is consistent with my theory. He has returned to the location of his earlier unsuccessful crime, in order to re-enact it successfully – over and over again."

"What do you intend to do, Lázár?" asked Sir Michael, his voice suddenly serious. "You cannot simply confront him."

"My plan is rather more subtle than that," said Count Erdélyi and proceeded to share it with them.

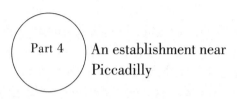

Part 4 An establishment near Piccadilly

I

THE DOOR OF THE HOUSE in Camden was opened by Silas Quinn himself. He peered past Count Erdélyi into the darkness pressing at his shoulder. "Were you followed?"

"I sincerely hope so."

"He took the bait?"

Count Erdélyi gave an ambivalent shrug.

"Will you come in?"

"I think it better that we proceed with the execution of our plan immediately, don't you? I have a motor taxi waiting."

"Allow me to get my cloak," said Detective Inspector Quinn.

Count Erdélyi turned and looked up at an anaemic moon.

II

They left the taxi in the gas-lit brightness of Piccadilly, with its crowds of drunks and pleasure-seekers, and turned into a dark side street. Silas Quinn led the way to an unmarked door, with so little hesitation that it seemed he must have been there before.

He gave the bell-pull three sharp tugs. As the door opened, the tinkle of a discordant piano and a burst of jagged laughter greeted them, along with the mixed aromas of alcohol, cigar smoke and cheap cologne. Another scent, altogether more animal, could also be discerned. The place smelled like any other bordello, in other words.

They were admitted by a 'madame' whose voice vibrated with an unexpected baritone depth, which caused Count Erdélyi to glance at her throat. A large Adam's apple protruded.

"Good evening, sirs. Please be so good as to follow me."

The 'madame' turned with an excessively feminine grace, and led the way with a swaying walk.

The shape of the body was sinuous and attractive, wrapped in the garishly-coloured silk of a kimono. If the count had not known better, he would have sworn he was following a woman.

The hall was narrow and poorly lit, so that they could form little impression of their surroundings. As they descended a flight of stairs into the basement, the smell of damp insinuated itself into the melée of other odours. The sound of the piano – it could not be called music – increased in volume.

The stairs gave directly onto a basement room, which served as some kind of bar. The table lamps were shaded in red, and clouds of smoke swirled around them. A dozen or so faces turned towards them as they entered. Their expressions betrayed their apprehensiveness, their sense of transgression. At first glance, the room was mostly comprised of men, with two or three overly made-up females amongst them. On closer examination, it was evident that these seeming-women were no more female than the 'madame' who had let them in. Masculine jaws and broad shoulders, together with a certain lack of elegance in their posture, gave the game away. Approximately half the group were middle-aged and dressed in evening suits and top hats. The other half, which included the 'women', were much younger and dressed more cheaply.

The 'madame' was now behind the bar. She turned invitingly towards Quinn and Count Erdélyi. "And what would you gentlemen care to drink?"

"It has to be champagne, I think," said Quinn. "A bottle of Dagonet, 1880, if you have it." Quinn turned his back on the bar as the bottle was fetched. "So, what do you think?"

"Of what?" answered Count Erdélyi uncertainly.

"Of our bordello. Would it surprise you to learn that fifty percent of the individuals here are policemen? I shall leave it to you to guess which half."

Count Erdélyi's jaw dropped as he looked around the room. "Not the prostitutes, I presume."

"You'd be surprised," was all that Quinn would say.

Count Erdélyi looked again, this time with narrowed eyes. It was true that some of the younger ones had a touch of the bobby about their features. He found himself pursing his lips appraisingly. "I am afraid there is a problem with your ruse. No one here is beautiful enough to tempt the Exsanguinist."

"You haven't seen Wendell yet," answered Quinn. "Will you ask Police Constable Wendell to come out, please?" he called over his shoulder.

III

Count Erdélyi felt a strange mixture of shame and humility as he examined the young man who was now presented to him. He felt himself to be base and ignoble, a creature of clay and crude passions, in comparison to the delicate beauty before him. He hardly dared look at the youth's face; yet he could not look away, for fear that the boy would have disappeared when he looked again, or that some essential quality of his beauty would be changed. The power of PC Wendell's beauty lay in the sense of its ephemerality, in its flower-like impermanence. This was not so much a human being, he felt, as the embodiment of a moment in a life. And when that moment had passed, the being that embodied it would be gone.

Wendell could not have been older than nineteen. His skin had a luminous clarity to it. His hair was blond, and flopped over his forehead in a soft fringe that had surely been permitted to grow longer than police regulations allowed. His eyes were a deep chestnut brown and his expression lacked any sense of awareness of the effect he had on others. Instead, his look communicated a simple eagerness for life and for action. Like many young men, he gave the impression of being in a hurry to make his mark on the world.

"What do you say now?"

Count Erdélyi kept his eyes on Wendell as he answered Quinn. "He is perfect."

IV

Quinn invited Wendell to join them at a table. A moment later, the 'madame' brought over an ice bucket with the champagne. They watched in silence as their host poured the amber liquid into tall flutes.

Count Erdélyi raised his glass with a sombre nod. He closed his eyes as he sipped. "A very fine vintage." He turned to Quinn with an ironic expression. "I am surprised your department permits such extravagances."

"It is not an extravagance. It is a necessary expense."

The count raised one eyebrow sceptically.

"According to the *De Profundis* letter, Dagonet

was Lord Alfred Douglas's favourite champagne," explained Quinn, "It is important to have a bottle out on display. It will act as a stimulus."

Count Erdélyi laid his glass down with careful precision. "I hardly think he needs stimulating. And doesn't it all rather depend on whether he shows himself here?"

"I believe the real Exsanguinist will not be able to resist confronting one he considers to be either an imposter or a rival. His curiosity surely must be piqued."

"And when he does show? What then?"

"We go along with whatever he suggests."

"Are there not dangers inherent in that course of action?"

"I'm not afraid," put in Wendell quickly. He spoke with a Cockney accent, full of bravado.

"Look around you," said Quinn. "We are surrounded by police officers."

"But what if he wants us to go elsewhere with him?"

"We must be prepared to improvise." Quinn drew apart his cloak and revealed a holstered revolver. "I am armed, and so is Wendell. We are both trained in the use of firearms."

"And if he doesn't show?"

"We offer him temptation."

"How do we do that?"

Detective Inspector Quinn glanced quickly at Wendell, a slight, uneasy smile playing on his lips.

V

"Tell me, Quinn. Has Constable Wendell been consulted in the role he is to play?"

"I understand what is expected of me," answered Wendell.

"And you're not afraid," completed the count, echoing Wendell's own words from a moment before. He gave the young man a kindly smile. "You know, I would feel better if you *were* a little afraid. It's natural and healthy and it might induce in you a degree of caution."

"The Inspector will look after me."

Quinn attempted a smile, but it came out as a grimace. If it was meant to be reassuring, it failed.

"This young man's life is your responsibility, Quinn. If he does not understand the danger to which he is about to be exposed, then you certainly do. If anything happens to him, you would be just as guilty as..."

Silas Quinn cut him off with a sharp gesture.

He dipped his head, causing Count Erdélyi to turn slowly. There at the entrance to the room stood Sir Michael Esslyn.

Even though he had clearly seen Count Erdélyi, the MP gave no greeting. To a careful observer, however, his determination to ignore the count was the surest indication that he had noticed him.

Sir Michael took a table on the opposite side of the room from theirs.

"We should ask him to join us," said Quinn.

"Shall I?" volunteered Count Erdélyi, half-rising.

"No. Let Wendell."

Constable Wendell gave a nod of assent and kicked back his chair. Count Erdélyi watched him cross to Sir Michael's table. Following Wendell's direction, Sir Michael looked across towards the count, his face lighting up theatrically. A moment later, he was at their table, with Wendell at his side.

"Lázár! I didn't see you! How extraordinary to find you here! Do you come here often?"

"I have never set foot in here before tonight. Will you join us, Michael? You remember Mr. Quinn."

"Of course," said Sir Michael, removing his

top hat and taking a seat. "Quinn, I have a bone to pick with you, so it is fortuitous that we should meet tonight."

Another glass appeared, and Sir Michael watched with a tense expression as his drink was poured. When the 'madame' had gone, Sir Michael leant forward and confided: "You know, I am convinced that some of the women here are not what they seem."

VI

"Is any one of us who we seem to be, Sir Michael?" replied Quinn provocatively.

Sir Michael's smile was almost flirtatious. "There you go again! You have a habit of making enigmatic comments. I cannot decide whether you really are the deeply mysterious being you seem to be or whether it is all a shallow affectation."

"I hope it is not the latter," said Quinn. "What was it that Oscar Wilde said? *The only sin is shallowness*'?"

"That seems typical of him, I must say. He hoped to impress through perversity. Brilliant words are all very well, but the brilliance sometimes distracts from the truth. He was a creator of marvellous surfaces, so it seems strange that he should decry shallowness."

"Do I take it that you are *not* an admirer of Wilde, Sir Michael?"

"Not remotely. Neither of his art nor his life."

"You surprise me."

"I don't see why it should surprise you. I am an MP, and a member of the Cabinet. I am hardly likely to be a supporter of a degenerate criminal."

"And yet you are here?"

"What is *here*?" asked Sir Michael.

"It is a place where men like you go in order to buy the sexual favours of boys like him," answered Quinn, indicating Wendell.

"Is it really?" answered Sir Michael, with a flat, calm tone. "I had no idea." He barely looked in Wendell's direction and gave the impression that he was not in the slightest bit interested in him.

"That's not why you came here?"

"No. I came here because... well, to be perfectly honest, I am not sure how I found myself here. I saw some other men come in and imagined it to be a different kind of establishment altogether."

"You were just passing and were – what? – curious? So you thought you would explore?"

"That's it. In a nutshell."

"What in particular engendered your curiosity, I wonder?"

"No doubt it was something about the faces of the men I saw enter. There was an appetite I recognised in their eyes. You might call it hunger. At the same time, they seemed to be expecting satisfaction. And so, I thought it was a restaurant. It's an easy mistake to make."

"Ah. You must be sorely disappointed."

"Yes."

"And yet, you have found your friend Count Erdélyi here. And me. A striking coincidence, isn't it?"

"Striking."

"One might even think you had followed us here."

"Why would I do that?"

"Well, you mentioned something about having a bone to pick with me."

"That's true. I really would like to talk to you about that. However, you must see that I cannot remain here. A man in my position cannot risk being discovered in such sordid surroundings. I wonder if we may not transfer to a less compromising locale? Would you object terribly, Quinn?"

"I don't object at all. My purpose in coming

here has been served. Where do you suggest we go?"

"It seems to me that anywhere would be less compromising than here. So let us go anywhere!" Sir Michael rose from the table, picking up his cane and top hat.

"Is it to be just you and I?" wondered Quinn, as if to delay Sir Michael. "Or shall the others join us?"

"Bring whomever you like. It really doesn't matter to me."

"What about him?" Quinn nodded towards Wendell. "Wouldn't you be sorry if he did not accompany us?"

Sir Michael Esslyn assessed the young man with pursed lips. "I can see that you are anxious to have him with us, so by all means..."

VII

The pursing of his lips turned into a satisfied smile. Then he turned and led the way out.

Wendell jumped up, charged with the energetic eagerness that seemed to characterise him. With a bow of the head to his commanding officer, he followed closely behind Sir Michael. Count

Erdélyi gave Quinn a hard look, silently reprising the warning he had issued earlier. Quinn rose to his feet and rushed to catch up with the other two.

The count was the last to emerge on the street. By the time he was on the scene it was too late for him to prevent or even understand what was happening. Sir Michael Esslyn was holding open the door of a taxi. Wendell and Quinn climbed in. Suddenly the taxi driver fired his engine and accelerated brutally, pulling the door out of Sir Michael's hand. The taxi's forward momentum caused the door to swing closed.

"What the devil!" cried Sir Michael. "Marchbanks!" he shouted after the taxi as it roared away and turned right into Piccadilly.

Count Erdélyi ran to the end of the dark alley and looked east, in the direction of Piccadilly Circus. The taxi had been engulfed in the flow of identical vehicles. He spun round and glared at Sir Michael, who was walking slowly up to him. "What's going on, Michael?"

"Don't get angry, old fellow. We cooked it up to help you – Toby Marchbanks and I. It's him driving the taxi, you see. The plan was to get a confession out of Quinn and then take him round to

New Scotland Yard. We didn't like the idea of you tackling him on your own. Too dangerous."

"I don't understand. What is Toby doing driving a taxi?"

"It's an eccentricity of his, I believe. He says he finds it useful for certain purposes. I can't imagine what."

"But why did he drive off like that?" asked Count Erdélyi.

"I have no idea," confessed Sir Michael. "It's not what we agreed at all."

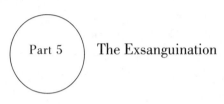

Part 5   The Exsanguination

I

SILAS QUINN WAS NOT A MAN to waste words on vain protests, or to demand explanations when it was clear that none would be given. In his line of work, success often depended on being able to surprise his adversary, and he had quickly concluded that the man driving the taxi was his adversary. He had heard Sir Michael's cry, so he knew the identity of the driver. All this was unexpected, he had to confess. But the surest way to ensure a positive result was to act as if nothing about this apparent abduction surprised him.

"Good evening, Lord Toby," he said calmly. "I am glad we have had this chance to renew our acquaintance."

The driver absorbed this in silence. There was a

slight movement of his head, a kind of spasm, but he did not turn round. His voice, when it came at last, was little more than a murmur, barely audible over the noise of the taxi engine. "Who are you, Quinn?"

"Your nemesis."

"That won't do." Lord Toby's voice rose to a high whine. "I don't believe in all that superstitious rot. There is no universal law that says a man must have a nemesis."

"Are there any universal laws at all, I wonder?"

"I know what you are trying to do." Lord Toby charged the words with bitterness.

"I assure you, all I am trying to do is to become better acquainted. Which reminds me, I do not believe you have been introduced to my friend, Sam Wendell."

"I'm not interested in him."

"You ought to at least look at him before you decide that. I think he is your type."

"You are confusing me with Pinky – or Lázár. I'm not like them. I'm engaged to be married."

"I'm not talking about your amorous inclinations." After a beat, Quinn added: "You know why I chose you."

"*You* chose *me*?"

"That's right. I chose you to help me."

"You cannot say you chose me!" Lord Toby squealed in outrage. "You did not choose this. You are not in control here. I am driving this vehicle. I will decide where we go, not you!"

"Yes, you are the master. I don't care where I go, as long as I go with you. It is an honour to be in your company. And I say that not because you're a member of the aristocracy, but because you're... why not say it? Because you are the Exsanguinist."

"I have never called myself that."

"No, but your acts have drawn the title onto you."

After a pause, Lord Toby said: "You will see what I am soon enough."

II

The taxi continued east along Shaftesbury Avenue and onto High Holborn. Silas Quinn settled back in his seat. Lord Toby seemed little inclined to talk, and so Quinn began a speculative monologue, trusting that Lord Toby would interrupt him whenever he got a detail wrong:

"When did it begin – the pain? When you stopped smoking opium? I have already said to you how courageous an act that was, to let the suffering back into your life. But perhaps I underestimated how much it cost you. Not only did you allow yourself to suffer physical agonies once more, but there were the memories too. Everything that you had escaped during the years of addiction now returned into your life."

The driver moved slightly, another twitch of agitation, but said nothing to contradict Quinn.

"The first one happened accidentally," continued Quinn. "A chance remark from a stranger, who just happened to cross your path, and all the rage and power that was in you was released. In that moment, your destiny was revealed to you. Your vocation, we might even call it. The first one, James Weston – but did you even know his name? A low-life, a prostitute, though pretty enough. I think I see what must have happened. He propositioned you. How dare he! What did he take you for? Some kind of degenerate? But you were engaged to be married! You were not the sort who consorted with renters."

Lord Toby let out a burst of tense laughter. "You're wrong, Quinn. I don't care about that. I have never judged Pinky, or Lázár for that matter. I understand that different men have different needs. Why should that provoke me?"

"But there is one thing you did care about, more than anything. With your emergence from opium addiction came the realisation of your loss. Your art! Utterly sacrificed! And for what? It all started when Sophie Armstrong fell pregnant with your child. You needed her out of the way, her and her unborn brat. No one could blame you for that. But fate had saved up a savage irony for you. Once you had accomplished your goal, you discovered you were no longer able to create. Your talent deserted you, along with your public. Tell me, when was all this? Seventeen, eighteen years ago? It's interesting to reflect that if the foetus had been allowed to go to full term and the child had been born – a boy, was it not? – he would have been about the age of James Weston the day you killed him. Was it that unborn child you killed then, and killed again, repeatedly? The child who had drained the life from your art – now you set yourself to drain the life from him."

A groan of suffering was Lord Toby's only answer.

"If art was your great ideal, then Oscar Wilde – the man who had attempted to turn his life into a work of art – was your hero. Somehow in the person of James Weston, the unborn child who had destroyed your creative impulses was merged with the sordid renters and the upper class homosexual lover who had destroyed Oscar. And the pain, the pain that you had felt on ending your addiction – suddenly you found deliverance from it. As the blade went into James Weston's throat, and his pain began, your pain eased."

"*Who are you, Quinn?*"

III

They had left Cheapside and the City behind them, and were now continuing east along Cable Street. "You are taking us to where it began," observed Quinn. "To Limehouse. James Weston's body was found in Limehouse, where no doubt he exercised his profession among the sailors who had become habituated to sodomy on their long sea voyages. Did you find yourself tempted by the opium dens you no longer allowed yourself to enter? And desperate for one form of consolation, which was now forbidden to you, you were unexpectedly presented with another?"

"I have allowed you to spout your defamatory nonsense," said Lord Toby through clenched teeth. "But I have admitted nothing."

"Nonsense? Why deny your genius? *The*

supreme vice is shallowness. Whatever is realized is right.' You took that as your moral as well as your artistic code. What else was it that Oscar Wilde said? *To deny one's own experiences is to put a lie into the lips of one's own life. It is no less than a denial of the soul.'* Do not deny your soul, I beg you!"

"What do you want from me?" The question was pulled from deep within Lord Toby. It seemed that at that moment he was afraid of Quinn.

"I want to learn from you."

"Why should I help you?"

"Because every great artist is a teacher. I can never hope to follow in your footsteps. But I can be the critic who explains you to the world. I can be Ruskin to your Turner." In that moment, as Quinn's eyes stared out almost enviously towards Lord Toby, it was hard to tell whether he was feigning his enthusiasm, or whether he was in truth as mad as the man he sought to trap.

Lord Toby took both hands off the wheel and pressed them to his temples. The taxi zig-zagged harmlessly; it was the only vehicle on the road at that time of night. If Quinn had hoped for some of his men to follow them, he was disappointed.

Lord Toby gripped the wheel again. "Soon

you'll understand everything. And there will be no need for any more words."

Quinn remained silent for the rest of the journey.

IV

They left the main road behind them, and the last of the street lights. The moon shivered above them, as white as a bone.

The beams of the taxi's headlights cut through the darkness, illuminating the desolate landscape of the area, the endless fields where bricks were manufactured, occasional firing-kilns rising like bottles half-buried in the ground. The acrid aftertaste of chemical processes hung in the air.

It seemed impossible that any human being could live here. The empty factories and towering chimneys that flashed momentarily into vision were themselves the residents, phantom-like and secretive. Then, unexpectedly, they entered a street of grim houses, some with broken windows, others closed up with wooden planks. The taxi came to a stop with a small explosion.

"Get out." Lord Toby's voice was menacingly quiet as he gave the command.

V

The house appeared to be abandoned. It no longer had its original door, but only a rough wooden board that was secured with a chain and heavy lock. Lord Toby had trouble with the lock, but eventually he pulled the board open and gestured for Quinn and Wendell to enter first.

They stepped into an impenetrable blackness. The dark seemed to contain invisible fingers that explored their faces and caressed their eyes. It held something else too: a fetid and penetrating odour, the stench of corruption.

There was a scraping sound and the flame of a match broke into the darkness. Lord Toby lit a lantern. Then he pulled the board closed, and secured it from inside with the same lock.

He turned to face Quinn. "The final mystery is oneself," he said.

Quinn recognised it as a quote from Wilde.

"Here is where I keep the mystery of myself."

Quinn looked around, frowning.

"It is here that I keep the blood," explained Lord Toby.

"The smell?" enquired Quinn.

"Blood is organic matter. It goes bad. I have

been collecting it for a long time now." Almost as an afterthought, he added: "Oh, and I have a boy downstairs, draining."

"Will you show him to us?"

"Of course. Why do you think I brought you here?"

VI

Lord Toby became suddenly self-conscious, almost timid, as he shone the light down into the cellar. His movements seemed constrained by a kind of reticent pride. Quinn realised that this was a crucial moment for him. He was like an artist about to reveal his masterpiece, half-afraid that it was not the great work he believed it to be, perhaps even more afraid that it was.

"Be careful. Some of the steps are missing." The solicitude of a murderer is strangely touching, realised Silas Quinn.

Wendell descended first, with his usual unthinking eagerness. Quinn followed, his feet cautiously exploring the darkness beneath him, arms forward so that he could feel the damp, crumbling bricks on either side.

Each step took him deeper into the stench of rotting blood.

The lantern was little help, its light obstructed by his own body. Whenever he reached a missing step, he always felt as if he was walking into an infinite abyss, that the next step would never come, and that he would plunge into the enveloping blackness.

Finally, when he was not expecting it, his foot touched something loose that he recognised as gravel. He was on the ground.

Wendell and Quinn instinctively kept close together as they waited for Lord Toby to join them. They looked up into the beam of his lantern, not daring to look behind them at whatever might be hidden in the darkness. The only indication of what was there was an irregular, liquid dripping sound that echoed coldly.

Lord Toby stepped between them and held the lantern high. They could not resist looking in the direction of its beam.

VII

The body was naked, and tied up with chains. Supernaturally pale, it was suspended from the ceiling by a single, thick chain: its wrists and ankles attached, the arc of the torso like an archer's bow. The lowest part of the body, the abdomen, almost touched the floor. The throat, which had been sliced open, gaped over a metal bucket.

Lord Toby moved the lantern and showed them the barrels of dark liquid that stood around the edges of the room.

Quinn looked back towards the suspended corpse. He saw a red droplet fall from the wound and join the bucket of blood below.

"Sin and suffering," said Lord Toby. "Beautiful, holy things."

"Modes of perfection," added Quinn.

"This is the most profound, the most perfect symbol ever created," remarked Lord Toby.

"But the smell," objected Quinn. "And this disgusting place. Do they not rather detract from the perfection?"

"But the smell is central to what I am seeking to create!" cried Lord Toby. "It is the stench of corruption. The body is cleansed and perfected by the draining of the blood, it becomes an object of art, rather than life. And the driving force of life is revealed to be a stinking mess of corruption."

Quinn nodded slowly, as if in dawning

comprehension. And perhaps he had finally understood the extent of Lord Toby's insanity.

"Do you approve of what I have done?"

"More than that. I revere it."

"Do you remember what you once said, Quinn? That it is not easy to kill someone. It was that comment that first interested me in you. I felt that you would be able to appreciate the enormity of my achievement. How difficult it has been for me to do this. You alone would understand what I have suffered for my art."

"I do."

"You asked for my help."

"Yes."

"I will help you. I will show you how to do it. How to kill."

There was a chair against one wall. Lord Toby crossed to it and put down the lantern. Something metallic glinted in the light.

Quinn looked uneasily towards Wendell. "Him?"

Lord Toby smiled strangely. He took down a brown bottle and a cloth from a high shelf. With the absorption of a creative artist, he opened the bottle and poured some of its contents into the cloth. The scent of ether joined the other smells of the cellar. He held the cloth out for Quinn to take.

Wendell's eyes flashed alarm; Quinn sought to reassure him with a look that he hoped inspired trust. But by now, Lord Toby had gripped the young policeman from behind. Wendell's resistance diminished as Quinn held the cloth over his face. Lord Toby eased his inert body to the ground.

"Shall I undress him?" said Quinn.

"This has nothing to do with him," answered Lord Toby. "This is between you and me. And for what is about to pass between us, there can be no witnesses."

Lord Toby began to undress.

VIII

His hand enclosed the object that had flashed metallically in the lantern beam. "A cut-throat razor. Like the one you once tried to use against your fellow-lodger all those years ago. Now is the time for you to abandon your scruples and to discover what you are capable of."

He came towards Quinn as if he would attack him, with the agility of a hunter. But at the final moment, he stopped and held the razor out, handle towards Quinn. As Quinn took the weapon, Lord Toby threw back his head, making his throat as large as he could. "Add my blood to the blood of my victims. Perfect me, as I perfected them."

"You? But why?"

"The pain always returns. The blade goes in, the pain eases. But it always returns. You will end the pain forever."

Quinn reached out and took the blade to the other man's throat. But the intimacy of the moment, the man's nakedness before him, the startling immediacy of his eyes, the soft, dark pleading of those eyes, robbed him of his courage.

"Must I make you practise on him first?" murmured Lord Toby, his lips barely moving.

Quinn tensed the muscles of his whole arm as he held the razor. And then he pushed with all his strength.

The blade must have been exceedingly sharp. It found the soft dip between the thyroid cartilage and the hyoid bone, and plunged into it. Quinn pushed the blade deeper with a cutting motion. Something dark disgorged from either side of it, and he felt a sense of immeasurable liberation.

There was a gurgling cry from the man at whose neck he was working, and then his body contorted and he fell forward. Quinn took the weight of his fall, and the majority of his blood. He held the man with one arm and lowered him gently to the floor. With his other hand, Quinn kept the razor pushed into Lord Toby's throat.

The dying man's eyes looked up at him and seemed to hold a smile.

In less than a minute the violent spasms of deep shock shook his body. Seconds after that, he was dead.

In the event, it had proved to be easier than Quinn had thought to kill someone.

There was a groan from the floor behind him. Quinn eased himself away from the dead man and turned his attention to Wendell.

The young man's eyes swam as he came round. The moment they focussed on Quinn, panic rose in them. Wendell tensed and backed away from his superior.

"It's alright," said Quinn. "He's dead. He attacked me with the razor, but I managed to overpower him. We got a full confession. The case is closed. You did well."

"I feel sick," said Wendell.

"That will be the ether. I'm sorry about that. But I felt it best to go along with him for as long as possible. As a precaution, I turned the cloth in my hand, so that you did not inhale the full force of the fumes. I would never have let you come to any harm, you know."

Wendell's lips pushed forward, as if in a pout, and then he vomited over himself: an appropriate response to Quinn's reassurances.

Quinn stood and held the razor up to examine it. He sniffed the fresh blood, which had a clarity to it that cut through the fetid atmosphere of the cellar.

For the first time in a long time, he felt complete.

If you enjoyed this book, don't miss the
other titles from the **paper planes** collection.

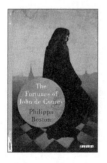

Here is an excerpt from:

Lilith

Alex Douglas

Chapter 1

I

"*I WANT U.*" the message read, "*Come 2 me.*"

William Clayborne shut his phone as his wife entered the kitchen. He hadn't seen the number the text originated from, but there was no need – only Lata was that direct. He looked at his watch: there was enough time for him to go via her place before his first class at the university. He finished his coffee in one gulp, and stood up.

"I have to get going."

"I thought you didn't start until ten on a Monday?" Sarah frowned, putting her bread in the toaster.

"Yeah... student papers to grade." he explained, picking up his bag, "I forgot to bring them home this weekend."

As he came to kiss her goodbye, Sarah raised her hand to his cheek, caressing it with her thumb.

"Bicycle *carefully*, baby." she instructed him, "And I love you."

"Me too." he smiled, kissing her goodbye.

II

William Clayborne had always had success with women. Nature had sculpted him a face with an apparently perfect combination of light and dark: sensitive and yet mysterious, as if he had experienced some secret tragedy. His undeniable intellect, with a doctorate in quantum mechanics and a research post at the university, completed the illusion of a man with a soul of rare profundity.

And an illusion it was: whatever women saw in him, whatever romantic potential they hoped to liberate, William did not feel it inside himself.

They were seduced by their own imaginations, and he was not to blame when the affair ended in disappointment. People will always see what they want to see.

I want u.

William smiled in anticipation as he bicycled down the hill.

The November sky was a perfect blue, the sunlight cutting the morning shadows with razor-sharp clarity. Passing under the trees, he moved from light to dark in rapid succession, the winter sun stroboscoping pleasurably on his eyes, almost hypnotic.

Come 2 me.

He suspected that Lata was falling in love with her idea of him, which was a problem. An unnecessary complication. William had noticed her in the very first class he gave this September, the class where each year he told his new students that they lived in an illusory world.

"At the sub-atomic level, the quantum level, there is *nothing* but electromagnetic radiation." he announced, looking over their faces, "The universe is pure energy. Nothing is solid. Nothing is fixed. The tables you are sitting at are only tables at our level of perception. They exist in this dimension, and this dimension alone."

His eyes fell upon Lata, watching him intently from the middle of the second row, one hand playing with her hair.

"Reality is like beauty." he said, fixing her with his gaze, "We all accept that beauty is subjective, a product of the way we perceive ourselves and the world around us. Beauty does not exist. It is just a value system: an order we impose on the world."

She'd let go of her hair and sat up straight.

"The table is part of a similar value system. We order, comprehend and *manipulate* electromagnetic radiation to create a dimension of tables... gardens... works of art... and girls with beautiful hair."

A small, embarrassed smile had crossed Lata's lips. William knew then that he had only to wait for her to come to him.

ABOUT THE AUTHOR

R.N. MORRIS is the author of a series of novels
featuring Porfiry Petrovich, the detective from
Dostoevsky's novel *Crime and Punishment*.
A Gentle Axe (2007) was followed by
A Vengeful Longing (2008), which was short-listed
for the CWA Dagger Award for best crime novel.
A Razor Wrapped in Silk comes out in April 2010.
(The series is published in France by 10/18.)
As Roger Morris, he wrote *Taking Comfort*,
published by Macmillan in 2006.
He has also written the libretto
for an opera about Jean Cocteau.
He lives in London with his wife and two children.
He has a website:
www.rogernmorris.co.uk

The Exsanguinist on www.paperplanes.fr:
• The audio version read by Les Clack
• R.N. Morris talks about writing *The Exsanguinist*
• More about Oscar Wilde and gentlemen's clubs